D0461631

You Were Loved

before you

were born

EVE BUNTING & KAREN BARBOUR

THE BLUE SKY PRESS • AN IMPRINT OF SCHOLASTIC INC. • NEW YORK

You Were Loved

BEFORE YOU

WERE BORN

Library of Congress catalog card number 2007009703.

ISBN-10: 0-439-04061-2 / ISBN-13: 978-0-439-04061-7

10 9 8 7 6 5 4 3 2 1   08 09 10 11 12

Printed in Singapore   46

First printing, January 2008

Designed by Kathleen Westray

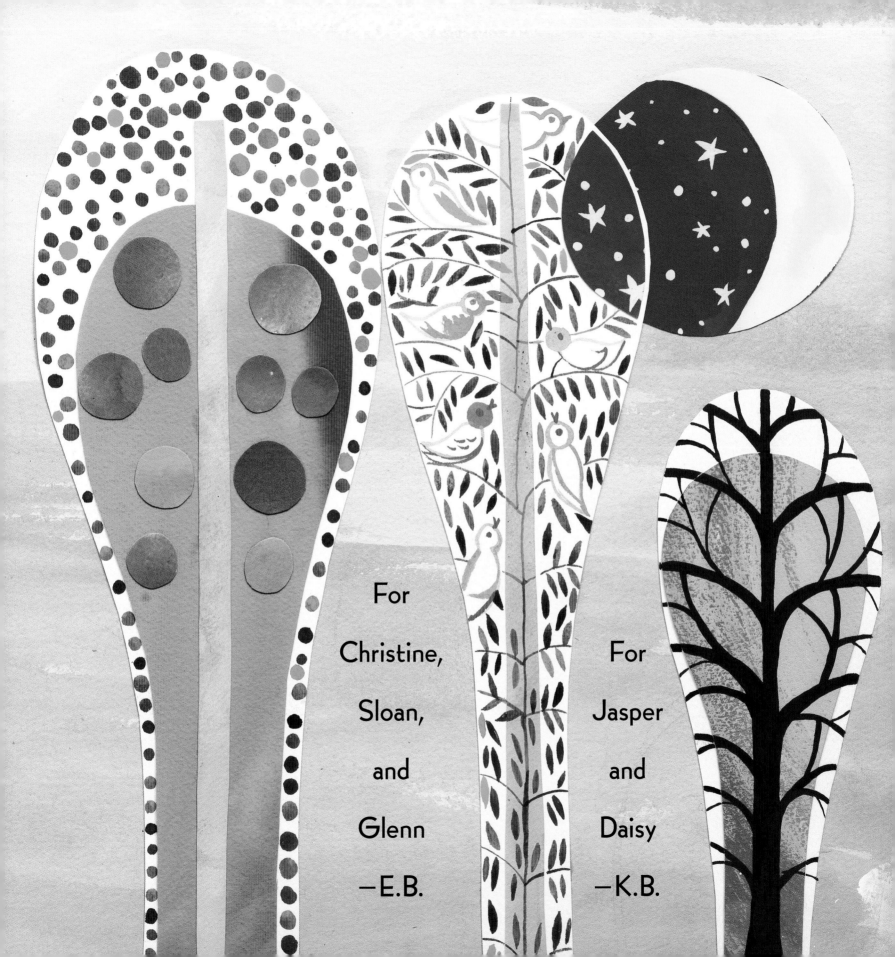

For
Christine,
Sloan,
and
Glenn
—E.B.

For
Jasper
and
Daisy
—K.B.

YOU WERE LOVED EVEN BEFORE YOU WERE BORN.

The minute

Daddy and I

found out

we were going

to have you,

we loved you.

Your grandmother planted a rosebush

in the garden that will grow

as you grow.

Your grandfather brought over this rocking chair. "I sat in it to rock your sister and then you," Grandma told me. "Now you will have your own baby to sing to and to hold."

Everyone helped get your room ready.

Before you were born,

you were loved by

your aunt. "I am giving

this child the moon

and the stars," she said.

"And a rainbow, too."

Your cousin helped his mom
sort clothes that had been
his when he was little.

He sent his four best baseball cards for you, too.

Your cousin loved you back then,

before he even saw you.

Our neighbor made

this butterfly kite for you.

"It will be a while

before the baby

will be big enough

to fly a kite," I told him.

"I can wait," he said.

The boys and girls in my dance class made this card for you. They brought it over. It was so big they had to edge it through the door.

And there were so many of them they
filled the living room, wall to wall.
They're coming to visit.

We told the dog

you'd be here soon.

WE WERE ALL WAITING.

And then . . .

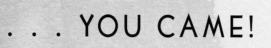

. . . YOU CAME!

You were loved by so many people

before you were born . . .

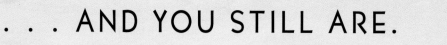

. . . AND YOU STILL ARE.